This book belongs to:

....

This book is for
Ethan James Percival

HarperCollins *Children's Books*

First published in paperback in Great Britain by HarperCollins Children's Books in 2011

10 9 8 7 6 5 4 3 2 1

ISBN: 978-0-00-734561-8

HarperCollins Children's Books is a division of HarperCollins Publishers Ltd.

Text and illustrations copyright © Tom Percival 2011

Visit our website at: www.harpercollins.co.uk

Printed in China

Hidden away at the bottom of a long forgotten garden,
lived a sad stray cat called Mr Tipps.

tweet

Nearly everyone is scared of *something*,
but poor Mr Tipps was scared of *everything*.

He worried about the wind that wailed...

donk!

and ran from the rain that soaked his fur.

Even his own shadow made him jump!

Poor Mr Tipps
wouldn't even dare
to climb a tree...

unless he **absolutely** had to!

And then he'd be too scared to come down again.

Early one morning,
Mr Tipps was
surprised to discover
a bowl of warm milk
waiting for him.

Peering around nervously,
he lapped up the milk and then darted away.

Every day after that
Mr Tipps found a
fresh bowl of milk,

and every day a young boy
crept a little closer...

until eventually...

the young boy and Mr Tipps became friends.

Sometimes, while his parents were busy,
the young boy and the stray cat would go exploring.

They flew kites,   played catch...

and watched the world go by.
Mr Tipps was **SO** happy, he forgot about being frightened.

But one day, there was no bowl.
No bowl, and no boy.

With a heavy heart,
Mr Tipps slipped
away down the
rain-soaked
street.

He hadn't gone far when suddenly a HUGE dog leapt out at him!

By the time he got away,
it was very dark and he was all alone.

The next morning,
when the sun rose,
Mr Tipps realised he
was completely lost.

He worried he might never find his way back home.

The young boy was worried too.

He'd rushed back from a weekend
at his grandmother's house
to leave out a bowl of milk...

but no one came to drink it.

The boy looked everywhere for Mr Tipps. He even put up notices...

but no one had seen the scruffy little cat.

Meanwhile, poor Mr Tipps was struggling to find his way home. He was cold, wet and miserable.

Just as he thought things couldn't get any worse, he was chased into a deep, dark wood.

The wind wailed through the gnarled old trees and rattled the twisty branches.

The cold night air was filled with strange and unnatural noises.

And that was when Mr Tipps saw it...

A terrifying monster rose out of the mist, huffing and puffing. It crept closer, and closer, and closer until...

"HOO

it shrieked.

Except it wasn't a monster at all...

just a young boy looking for his lost cat.

So, together, the friends made their way home.

Now that Mr Tipps had somewhere safe to live
and enough to eat, he completely forgot to be scared...

Although he never did get the hang of climbing down trees!